Buffy THE VAMPIRE SLAYER™

Spike and Dru

based on the television series created by
JOSS WHEDON

writers **CHRISTOPHER GOLDEN**
and **JAMES MARSTERS**

artists **RYAN SOOK** and **ERIC POWELL**

with **DREW GERACI, KEITH BARNETT, ANDY KUHN,**

HOWARD SHUM, and **NORMAN LEE**

colorist **GUY MAJOR**

letterer **PAT BROSSEAU**

These stories take place in the twentieth century

Titan Books

"all's fair"
by CHRISTOPHER GOLDEN and ERIC POWELL
with DREW GERACI, KEITH BARNETT, ANDY KUHN,
HOWARD SHUM, and NORMAN LEE

"the queen of hearts"
by CHRISTOPHER GOLDEN and RYAN SOOK

"paint the town red"
by JAMES MARSTERS, CHRISTOPHER GOLDEN, and RYAN SOOK

"who made who?"
by CHRISTOPHER GOLDEN and ERIC POWELL
with KEITH BARNETT and DREW GERACI

publisher
MIKE RICHARDSON

editor
SCOTT ALLIE
with BEN ABERNATHY, ADAM GALLARDO, and MICHAEL CARRIGLITTO

designers
KEITH WOOD and KRISTEN BURDA

art director
MARK COX

special thanks to
DEBBIE OLSHAN at FOX LICENSING and
CAROLINE KALLAS and GEORGE SNYDER at BUFFY THE VAMPIRE SLAYER

PUBLISHED BY
TITAN BOOKS
144 SOUTHWARK STREET
LONDON SE1 0UP

what did you think of this book? we love to hear from our readers. please email us at:
readerfeedback@titanemail.com, or write to us at the above address.

FIRST EDITION
JULY 2001
ISBN: 1 - 84023 - 282 - X

1 3 5 7 9 10 8 6 4 2

printed in Italy.

Art by RYAN SOOK
Colors by GUY MAJOR

<FOREIGNERS! DEMONS!>

<YOU KILLED MY GRAND-DAUGHTER!>

BUGGER OFF, OLD MAN. AND KEEP IT DOWN, RIGHT? WE'RE BRITISH *AND* WE'RE VAMPIRES-- THAT'S TWO STRIKES AGAINST US IF WE'RE DISCOVERED.

<VAMPIRE! YOU KILLED HER-- ARRGHHH!>

<YOU'RE NOT BEING VERY NICE. AFTER ALL, WHAT WERE WE TO DO? XIN RONG WAS THE SLAYER. IT WAS A MATTER OF SELF-PRESERVATION. NOTHING PER-SONAL.>

<YOU... YOU TORE HER APART! RIPPED HER BODY UP AND SCATTERED THE PIECES!>

<YEAH, WELL, YOU GOT US THERE. THAT BIT WAS JUST FOR FUN.>

<I WILL SEE YOU DEAD!>

<STOP THE FOREIGN DEMONS! THEY SLAUGH-TERED MY-->

<EH? AT LAST, YOU'VE COME. YOUR SISTER... THEY KILLED HER. WE MUST FIND THEM, DESTROY THEM...>

<WE SHALL, GRANDFATHER. XIN RONG WILL BE AVENGED. NO MATTER HOW LONG IT TAKES.>

CHICAGO, ILLINOIS, 1933. THE WORLD'S FAIR. A HYMN SUNG IN THE NAME OF THE GREAT GOD PROGRESS. THE FUTURE ON DISPLAY FOR ALL TO SEE.

SCIENCE. TRANSPORTATION. GOVERMENT. COMMUNICATIONS. ENERGY. THE EXPLORATION OF WORLD CULTURES. IT IS A SPECTACLE UNLIKE ANY OTHER...

FOR FOLKS FROM CHICAGO AND THE ILLINOIS COUNTRYSIDE, IT IS PERHAPS THE MOST AMAZING SIGHT ANY OF THEM HAVE EVER SEEN.

BUT IT IS ALSO A MECCA FOR TOURISTS ACROSS AMERICA, AND EVEN AROUND THE WORLD. YES, THEY'VE COME FROM ALL OVER TO BE HERE.

EVERYBODY WANTS TO GO TO THE FAIR.

IS IT EVERYTHING YOU THOUGHT IT'D BE, DRU?

BETTER. LIKE BEING INSIDE A DIAMOND. I'VE NEVER BEEN ANYWHERE SO SPARKLY. IT GIVES ME SHIVERS.

WANT TO HAVE A BIT OF FUN, THEN? ELICIT SOME PAIN AND SUFFERING, MAYBE GET AN ICE CREAM?

THOUGHT YOU'D NEVER ASK.

spike & dru

ALL'S FAIR

ISN'T IT AMAZING, NORA?

I'LL SAY. I FEEL LIKE ALICE IN WONDERLAND. MY LORD, WHO WOULD EVER HAVE THOUGHT WE WOULD LIVE IN A WORLD WHERE SUCH THINGS ARE POSSIBLE?

WELL, NOW I GUESS I'VE SEEN EVERY-THING.

NOT QUITE.

WHEN YOU'VE SEEN YOUR OWN BLOOD SPRAY YOUR WIFE'S FACE, THEN WATCHED MY SWEETHEART LICK IT OFF LIKE THE DARLING PUPPY SHE IS? *THEN* YOU'VE SEEN EVERYTHING.

SSSHH, MY SWEET PET. IT'S ALL RIGHT. DON'T FRET NOW. IT'S THE WAY OF THINGS. HOLLOW BONES AND FAILING EYES. THE MOON SCREAMS AND IT'S OVER. NO ONE LIVES FOREVER.

THIS IS RIDICULOUS, SAM. WE CAN'T JUST PRETEND IT DIDN'T HAPPEN. PEOPLE HAVE A RIGHT TO KNOW.

GUY'S PROBABLY LONG GONE, EDDIE. NEVER MIND HOW FAST THE TOURISTS WOULD CLEAR OUT IF THEY KNEW. UNLESS YOU WANT THE GOVERNOR AS AN ENEMY, YOU'LL KEEP QUIET.

LADIES AND GENTLEMEN, I PRESENT TO YOU AN INVENTION THAT WILL CHANGE THE WORLD.

IMAGINE AN ENDLESS POWER SOURCE. ODORLESS, SMOKE-LESS, SIMPLE TO USE, AND BEST OF ALL, FREE!

USING THIS MACHINE, I CAN CONVERT THAT ENERGY TO POWER. IMAGINE, IF YOU WILL, LIGHT BULBS THAT NEVER BURN OUT, AN AUTO-MOBILE THAT NEVER NEEDS GASOLINE.

USING THE MACHINE YOU SEE BEFORE YOU, I HAVE MANAGED TO TAP INTO AN ALTERNATE DIMEN-SION, A PARALLEL WORLD BEYOND OUR UNIVERSE WHOSE VERY SUBSTANCE IS RAW ENERGY.

IMAGINE THE WORLD'S INDUSTRIES RUN ON SAFE, CLEAN FUEL THAT COSTS NOTHING! IMAGINE HOW QUICKLY TECH-NOLOGY WILL PROGRESS THEN!

IMAGINE HOW EMPTY-HEADED AND FOOLISH SOME-ONE WOULD HAVE TO BE TO BELIEVE A LINE OF MALARKEY LIKE THAT! BAH. ALTERNATE DIMENSIONS, ENERGY FROM BEYOND THE UNIVERSE.

YOU'VE GONE TOO FAR, THIS TIME, PROFESSOR BRRRON. THIS CHARADE IS THE LAST STRAW. WHAT'VE YOU GOT IN THERE, A TINY GENERATOR OR SOMETHING?

NO, GENTLEMEN, PLEASE. I SWEAR TO YOU, IT'S THE TRUTH. THERE'S INFINITE POWER BEYOND THE VEIL OF THIS WORLD, IF WE ONLY ACCESS IT. PLEASE, IF YOU LOOK HERE YOU'LL SEE--

WE'VE SEEN ENOUGH, BARRON. CONSIDER YOURSELF LUCKY WE DON'T ASK THE FAIR ORGANIZERS TO EJECT YOU.

NO, WAIT, PLEASE. IF YOU'LL JUST LET ME SHOW YOU...

SMALL-MINDED FOOLS. I COULD CHANGE THE WORLD, BUT THEY REFUSE TO BELIEVE.

PAUL. OH, I'M SORRY PAUL, I KNOW HOW HURT YOU MUST BE. BUT... DON'T YOU THINK YOU SHOULD GO AFTER THEM? THEY COULD RUIN YOU.

OH, BRIDGET DARLING, DON'T WORRY. I KNOW YOU MUST BE ANXIOUS. IF WE'RE TO MARRY, I MUST HAVE A MEANS OF SUPPORTING OUR FAMILY. BUT THOSE MEN ARE FOOLS.

I LOVE YOU, PAUL, AND I BELIEVE YOU. YOU'LL FIND A WAY.

I WILL, DEAR. I SWEAR TO YOU. I HAVE CRACKED THE SHELL OF ANOTHER REALM, TAPPED THE FURNACE OF ITS HEART.

ONE WAY OR ANOTHER, I WILL USE THAT KNOWLEDGE TO CHANGE THE WORLD.

AAIIEEEEE! NO! DON'T TOUCH ME!

NOT UNTIL YOU GIVE US A KISS, POODLE.

YOU THERE! PUT THAT WOMAN DOWN THIS INSTANT.

SORRY, OFFICER. JUST HAVING A BIT OF FUN, LIKE. NO HARM DONE.

OFF WITH YOU, THEN. AND NO MORE SHENANIGANS. YOU'RE WASTING MY TIME.

HEE HEE. WHAT A CRANKY OLD GIT HE WAS. GOT LITTLE NIBBLY BUGS IN HIS HEAD, I THINK. CAN'T A GIRL HAVE A BIT OF A TUMBLE WITH HER MAN?

THEY'RE ON EDGE, DRU. A LITTLE CRANKY. NOT AS IF WE DIDN'T GIVE THEM REASON TO BE AFTER LAST NIGHT. WE'D BEST TAKE CARE, TONIGHT. DOESN'T MEAN WE CAN'T STILL HAVE FUN.

HERE WE ARE, THEN. ALL THESE EXHIBITS AROUND, WE MIGHT AS WELL DO A BIT OF EXPLORIN', MAYBE LEARN SOMETHING, EH? THE FAIR AIN'T ALL BLOOD AND POPCORN, Y'KNOW.

OOH, I LIKE IT HERE. WE FINALLY FOUND SOMETHING OLDER THAN WE ARE.

Exact Dinosaur Replica

MMMMMM.

DRU, WHAT IS IT? YOU ALL RIGHT, PET?

OH, NO NOT AT ALL. I CAN FEEL THEM ALL 'ROUND US, WATCHING. HATE SO UGLY AND DARK. TAKE ME AWAY.

ALL RIGHT, DRU. BUT WHERE? YOU HAD A LITTLE VISION, OR JUST SENSED SOMETHING?

I CAN FEEL THEM, SPIKE. I'M ALL SHUDDERY, DIRTY WITH THEIR EYES. TAKE ME OUT.

WE'RE GOING, POODLE. I DON'T SEE A DAMN THING, BUT WE'RE GOING.

MARVEL, LADIES AND GENTLEMEN, AT A MIRACLE OF THE FUTURE.

SIMPLE AS TAPPING A KEG OF BEER, I HAVE BROKEN THROUGH TIME AND SPACE, FROM THIS DIMENSION INTO ANOTHER, TO FIND INFINITE ENERGY.

EVEN A CASUAL VIEWER, ONE UNSCHOOLED IN THE SCIENCES, CAN WITNESS UP CLOSE THE ENERGY PRODUCED BY MY GENERATOR.

WITNESS LADIES AND GENTLEMEN, AS THE POWER SURGES, A CHARGE PRODUCED NOT BY ANY MECHANICAL MEANS...

...NOR ELECTRICITY-- QUITE SIMPLY, RAW POWER COLLECTED IN A BATTERY WITHIN THE GENERATOR, A CONSTANT FLOW PROVIDING CONSTANT POWER.

YEAH? IF THIS THING'S FOR REAL, THEN WHAT THE HELL ARE YOU DOING HERE WHEN YA OUGTTA BE A MILLIONAIRE?

WHAT I AM DOING HERE, AS ANY IDIOT CAN SEE, IS TRYING TO GIVE THE WORLD THE GREATEST SCIENTIFIC REVELATION IN HISTORY. BUT NARROW-MINDED FOOLS ARE ALL I SEE.

RATHER THAN BEING REVERED FOR MY ACHIEVEMENT, I AM FORCED TO DEAL WITH NEANDERTHALS SUCH AS YOURSELF WHO DON'T DESERVE TO REAP THE BENEFITS OF MY INVENTION!

OOOH. IT'S LIKE WATCHING ANGELS DANCE...

...WHILE THEY BURN.

THEY GO UP LIKE KINDLING, DON'T THEY? WHAT DO YOU WANT TO DO NEXT, LOVE?

THE PANTHEON DE GUERRE. A WHOLE BUILDING DEDICATED TO WAR AND DEVASTATION. LET'S GO SEE IT.

BY ALL MEANS. WHAT DO YOU THINK, THOUGH? WANT TO HAVE A BITE TO EAT FIRST?

WHO'D YOU HAVE IN MIND?

YEARRRR! A BLEEDIN' GHOST IN THE SHADOWS, RIGHT? SEE IF YOU CAN FLY!

THUNK

LET'S KILL THEM ALL. HUMAN, DEMON, SHADOW CREATURES. I CAN SMELL THEIR BLOOD AND IT SHRIEKS TO BE FREE.

NICE IN THEORY, DRU, BUT DID YOU GET A HEAD COUNT? WE DON'T KNOW WHAT WE'RE UP AGAINST, OR HOW MANY THERE ARE.

TO ME, THAT SAYS RE-TREAT.

HANG ON TIGHT.

WHO THE HELL *ARE* THESE GUYS?

THIS WAY!

OR MAYBE NOT THAT WAY. COME ON, DRU. I THINK I SEE A WAY OUT OF HERE.

THE WASPS IN MY HEAD ARE ANGRY, SPIKE. WHY ARE WE RUNNING?

WE'RE RUNNING 'CAUSE THEY GOT THE DROP ON US, WE'RE OUTNUMBERED, THEY'VE GOT NASTY WEAPONS, AND THEY MOVE FASTER THAN ANYONE I'VE EVER SEEN.

THUNK
THUNK

KRAASH

MARVELOUS. APPARENTLY OUR VACATION ISN'T QUITE OVER YET.

LOOK, SPIKE, ISN'T IT BEAUTIFUL? AS THOUGH THE HEAVENS BUILT THE STARS A HOME.

DRU? FOCUS, PLEASE.

<SPIKE. AT LAST. THIRTY YEARS WE TRAINED IN THE WAY OF THE WARRIOR AND THE PATH OF SHADOWS SO THAT YOU COULD BE MADE TO SUFFER. THREE YEARS WE HAVE HUNTED YOU.>

<AND NOW WE HAVE YOU.>

ALL RIGHT, FOLKS. NOTHING TO SEE HERE. THE FAIR IS CLOSED, SO JUST GO ON HOME.

YOU MUST UNDERSTAND, PAUL, IT WASN'T HER BLOOD WE WANTED. IT WAS HER PAIN. YOUR BETRAYAL OPENED THE WAY, AND THE GREAT OLD ONES RETURN.

YOU HAVE CREATED THE DOOR. NOW, AFTER EONS, THIS WORLD IS OURS ONCE AGAIN.

RIGHT, THEN. WELL DONE. YOU'VE GOT ME RIGHT WHERE YOU WANT ME, YEAH? MIND TELLING ME WHAT EXACTLY IT IS I'M SUPPOSED TO HAVE DONE TO PISS YOU OFF?

HER NAME WAS XIN RONG. SHE WAS THE SLAYER. SHE WAS OUR SISTER. YOU KILLED HER.

HISSSSS

WHAT, THAT LITTLE TART DURING THE BOXER REBELLION?

WHAT WAS THAT, 1900? RIGHT, NOW I REMEMBER HER. LOT OF FUN, THAT GIRL...

...I CAN STILL TASTE HER.

SNAP

DRU...

MOVE!

KRAASH

THIS WAY!

WELL. HMPH. I'M NOT HAVING FUN ANYMORE. SPIKE, LET'S SUCK THE MARROW FROM THEIR BONES.

EXCELLENT PLAN, DRU. WE'LL GET RIGHT 'ROUND TO THAT IF WE MANAGE TO STAY ALIVE. WE'RE IN A BIT OF A JAM IF YOU HADN'T NOTICED. WHAT NEXT?

BOOM!

Y'KNOW, SOMETIMES THE GODS ARE JUST ON OUR SIDE. THE CRUEL ONES OF COURSE.

REMEMBER THAT SCIENTIST-BLOKE? THE ONE WITH THE CHAOS-ENGINE?

I REMEMBER. LOOKS LIKE HE'S MADE A BIT OF A MESS OF THINGS, HASN'T HE?

I'D SAY SO. I'D ALSO CALL HIM OUR NEW BEST FRIEND.

YOUR THIRST FOR POWER AND KNOWLEDGE CALLED TO US, PAUL BARRON. YOU TOUCHED THE REALM OF THE ELDER GODS WITH YOUR PETTY SCIENCE, AND WE ANSWERED.

THIS IS BUT THE BEGINNING. YOU WILL CREATE ANOTHER MACHINE, ONE THAT WILL OPEN A RIFT TO DARK BEYOND LARGE ENOUGH THAT THE OLDEST AMONG US MIGHT STEP THROUGH.

YOU ARE THE CHOSEN ONE, PAUL BARRON. OUR HARBINGER. YOU WILL NOT FAIL US, DO YOU... EH?

YOU DARE MUCH, VAMPIRE, INTRUDING UPON US NOW.

RIGHT, YEAH. HEY THERE. LOOK, WELCOME ABOARD AND ALL THAT. WE CAUGHT AN EYEFUL OF THAT CHAOS SURGE JUST BLASTED THE ROOF OFF? FIGURED WE'D DROP IN.

IN FACT, WE WERE HOPING WE COULD JOIN THE PARTY. Y'KNOW, MAKE AN OFFERING OF FLESH AND BLOOD AND SOULS, SWEAR AN OATH OF FEALTY, ALL THAT SORT OF THING.

LOOK, SPIKE...I THINK IT LIKES ME.

WELL WHO WOULDN'T, LOVE.

SO WHAT'S IT TO BE?

BOOM!

DRU, PET, YOU WERE AMAZING. NEVER SEEN YOU SO VICIOUS. GOT ME A BIT HOT UNDER THE COLLAR.

YOU ALWAYS KNOW JUST WHAT TO SAY.

OH, POOR THING. BAD SPIKE, YOU BROKE HIS TOY. HOW WILL WE MAKE IT UP TO HIM?

I WAS SUPPOSED TO CHANGE THE WORLD.

SSSHH, IT'S ALL RIGHT, BABY. AUNTIE DRU'S GOT A LITTLE SURPRISE FOR YOU. WHEN I'M DONE, YOU CAN PLAY WITH YOUR TOYS AND THOSE NASTY OLD GODS ANY TIME YOU LIKE ...FOREVER.

NOT SURE THAT WAS THE BEST OF IDEAS, DRU, TURNING HIM. WHAT IF HE DOES MANAGE TO OPEN ANOTHER DOOR, CALL THE GREAT OLD WANKERS DOWN? THEY'LL BE A BIT TICKED AT US, I'D SAY.

WE'LL JUST HAVE TO MAKE SURE WE'RE NOT AROUND WHEN IT HAPPENS. DON'T WORRY, HE'LL BE A GOOD PUPPY. I'LL TRAIN HIM.

D'YOU FANCY A BITE, SPIKE?

YOU JUST ATE.

I KNOW, BUT I LIKED HIM. COULDN'T WE RIP SOMEONE INTO TINY BITS?

WHAT-EVER YOU WANT, DRU. ANYTHING FOR MY BABY.

THE END

SOUTHERN ILLINOIS. HEADING WEST. HEADING, EVENTUALLY, TO A SMALL CALIFORNIA TOWN WITH MORE THAN ITS SHARE OF DARKNESS. BUT THAT'S FOR LATER.

THIS IS NOW.

♪ ONCE I WAS GLAD, ALWAYS HAPPY, NEVER SAD. ♪

♪ AND EVERY DAY, SEEMED LIKE SUNDAY... ♪

♪ OH, THE QUEEN OF HEARTS, I DON'T KNOW WHERE TO START... OR HOW TO STOP... ♪

THERE'S SUCH PAIN IN THIS MUSIC, SPIKE. IT'S PURE BLISS.

YEAH, WELL, THE BLUES ALWAYS DID MAKE YOU HAPPY, PET.

IT'S LIKE THE MEMORY OF TEARS, WITHOUT THE SALTY TASTE. EVER SO DELICIOUS.

IT'S GOT ME FAMISHED, SPIKE. I CAN'T HEAR THE STARS WHEN I'M HUNGRY. WOULDN'T YOU FANCY STOPPING FOR A BITE?

ALL RIGHT, DRU. BUT A QUICK ONE, YEAH? JUST A LITTLE SOMETHING TO TIDE US OVER, MAYBE EVEN GET SOMETHING ON THE RUN.

OH, GOODY...

AAAAH! BLOODY HELL, DRU!

SKRREEEE

WHY'D YOU WANT TO GO AND DO A THING LIKE THAT?

I TOLD YOU I WAS HUNGRY, DADDY. AND NOW YOU'RE CROSS. I'VE BEEN NAUGHTY, BUT I CAN'T HELP MYSELF.

I'M NOT CROSS, DRU, JUST BLEEDING, IS ALL. AND I SAID WE'D GET A BITE. IF WE DON'T PASS A HITCHHIKER SOON, WE'LL STOP WHEN WE GET TO ST. LOUIS, ALL RIGHT?

YOU LIKE IT WHEN I'M NAUGHTY. I CAN TELL. THERE ARE DRAGONS IN YOUR EYES.

WHOOOOOOO

WHOOOOOOOOO

WELL NOW, ISN'T THIS MARVELOUS? WHO SAYS THERE'S NEVER A COP AROUND WHEN YOU NEED ONE?

THEY HAVE THE MOST DELICIOUS CHOCOLATE TORTES IN VIENNA. WHAT WAS THE NAME OF THAT SHOP? DO YOU REMEMBER?

GERSTNER'S. IT WAS GERSTNER'S.

I SUPPOSE YOU'RE GOING TO TELL ME YOUR SPEEDOMETER IS BROKEN. THAT YOU DIDN'T REALIZE YOU WERE DRIVING NEARLY NINETY MILES AN HOUR, AND THAT YOU SWERVED 'CAUSE THERE WAS A BEE IN THE CAR.

SEE WHAT YOU DO TO ME, POODLE?

GHURRK!

SKREEEE!

SPIKE & DRU

QUEEN OF HEARTS

MMMMMM...

I LOVE YOU QUEEN OF HEARTS ...I DON'T KNOW WHERE TO START... OR HOW TO STOP...

ST. LOUIS, MISSOURI. GATEWAY TO THE WEST.

MR. KING?

SIR, THIS IS VALERIE DUCLOS. SHE'S HAVING A RUN OF EXCELLENT LUCK THIS EVENING. MS. DUCLOS, MAY I INTRODUCE ZACHARIAH KING, OWNER OF THE QUEEN OF HEARTS.

A PLEASURE TO MEET YOU, MS. DUCLOS. I'M PLEASED TO HEAR OF YOUR SUCCESS AT THE TABLES TONIGHT. WOULD YOU CARE TO JOIN ME FOR A CELEBRATORY COCKTAIL?

WOULD I CARE TO... THAT WOULD BE WONDERFUL. YOU KNOW, I'VE NEVER WON ANYTHING IN MY LIFE BEFORE TONIGHT. MAYBE MY LUCK IS IMPROVING.

UNDOUBTEDLY.

IT'S THE RIVER, I THINK. SHE HAS POWER AND MAJESTY UNEQUALLED ON EARTH, AND SOMETIMES, SHE SHARES IT WITH THE REST OF US.

IT BURNS THE WORLD, IT'S SO ANGRY... IT'S A BAD SUN.

FIGHTS SO HARD, POSTURES AND ROARS ITS BRAVADO. LISTEN TO IT ROAR, SPIKE. SO ANGRY, BUT FILLED WITH MORE DESPAIR THAN DROWNING LOVERS.

EMPRESS

IT'S WHIMPERING NOW. TERRIBLY SAD, REALLY. DAY AFTER DAY, IT PUFFS ITS CHEST WITH POWER AND PRIDE.

YET NIGHT AFTER NIGHT, THE DARK GRAPPLES WITH THE POOR SUN, WRESTLING IT DOWN, SUFFOCATING IT. *KNOWS* IT'LL LOSE, BUT EVERY MORNING IT HAS HOPE THAT THE NEXT TIME WILL BE DIFFERENT.

GOTTA TELL YA, PET...

THE SUN SOUNDS LIKE A BLOODY MORON TO ME.

I DON'T MIND LOSING, AS LONG AS EVERYBODY'S PLAYIN' FAIR.

OOH, SO SPARKLY. I'M FEELING RED, SPIKE. RED AS THE SKY, RED AS THE OCEAN.

RIGHT, THEN. LUCKY THIRTEEN, IN MY GIRL'S FAVORITE COLOR.

KISS THEM FOR LUCK, SPIKE. PRAY TO THE UGLIEST OF DARK ONES FOR IT. NO ONE EVER PRAYS TO THEM, SO THEY HAVE LOTS OF WISHES TO GO AROUND.

LUCK.

SEVEN!

YOU DID IT, LOVE. YOU KEEP THIS UP AND WE'LL OWN THIS BARGE BY DAWN.

"YOU REALLY ARE MY LADY LUCK."

OH, SO PRETTY. I CAN SEE ALL OF MY SELVES IN THE GLASS.

GO ON, THEN, GIVE US ANOTHER.

AND AGAIN.

EXCUSE ME, MISS. NOT TO INTERRUPT YOUR DANCING, BUT THE OWNER OF THE CASINO, MR. KING, WANTED TO MEET YOU, CONGRATULATE YOU ON YOUR WINNINGS.

I CAN FEEL THE RIVER UNDER US. AND THE ONE UNDER THAT, THE LUCK FLOWS WITH THEM, LIKE THE MOON AND THE TIDES. DO YOU FEEL THEM?

MISS?

OH, I DON'T THINK SO. HE'S GOT A BIT OF BLOOD UNDER HIS NAILS, HASN'T HE? I DON'T LIKE PEOPLE WHO HIDE. I USUALLY RIP THEIR FACES OFF.

QUEEN OF HEARTS.

BLOODY HELL!

I SEE YOU, GREEDY LITTLE THING, HIDING YOUR FACE. I SEE YOU.

COME ON, DRU. OUR LUCK'S TURNED.

"...LET'S SEE IF WE CAN'T FIND SOME OTHER FUN."

TEN BUCKS COVER, CASE YA DIDN'T HEAR ME THE FIRST TIME.

THAT'S EACH. TEN... EACH...

COME ON, LOVE, STOP DILLY-DALLYING AND LET'S GET ON WITH IT.

YOU SHOULDN'T BE STRAINING YOURSELF, ANYWAY. YOU KNOW YOU'RE NOT WELL.

COME ON, SPIKE. I HAVE TO HAVE *SOME* FUN. ANYWAY, I *LIKE* THIS ONE. HE HAS MAGGOTS IN HIS BRAIN. THEY'RE CHEWING IN THERE, AND IT TASTES LIKE MANGOES.

YOU'VE GOT SHADOWS ON YOUR EYES, SPIKE. AREN'T YOU HAVING FUN?

TRYING, PET. JUST A BIT OFF IS ALL. WE WERE WINNING TONIGHT, AND IT ALL WENT TO HELL. SORT OF SOURED EVERY-THING.

HE MADE YOU LOSE. SAW HIS OTHER FACE, I DID. MADE ME SHUDDER. THOUGHT HE'D HAVE *ME* FOR DINNER, AND NOW HE'S MADE YOU SAD.

WHAT ARE YOU SAYING, DRU? SOME WANKER *MADE* ME LOSE?

I SAW BOTH HIS FACES. TWO FACES, JUST LIKE THERE'S TWO RIVERS, ONE UNDER THE OTHER. LIKE THE SHADOWS IN THE DARK.

HE'S A NASTY MAN, SPIKE. WE CAN GO BACK IF YOU LIKE. WOULD IT MAKE YOU HAPPY TO KILL HIM?

LIKE IT WAS CHRIST-MAS MORNING, PET.

...BEEN VERY LUCKY TONIGHT. PERHAPS YOU'D CARE TO JOIN ME FOR A CELEBRATORY DRINK?

MR. KING, SIR?

WHAT IS IT?

HE'S BACK, SIR, THE MAN YOU ASKED US TO WATCH FOR.

AND HE'S WINNING AGAIN.

WELL, WELL, I THOUGHT HE WAS A BOLD ONE.

BRING HIM TO MY ROOMS.

KA-PLINK

SEVEN BLACK. NO WINNERS.

THAT'S ALL RIGHT. I THINK I'VE GOT WHAT I CAME FOR NOW.

I'VE BEEN ASKED TO INFORM YOU THAT MR. KING, OWNER OF THE QUEEN OF HEARTS, REQUESTS YOUR COMPANY IN HIS PRIVATE QUARTERS.

WELL, NOW, I'M NOT THAT KIND OF GIRL, BOYS, BUT WHAT THE HELL, LEAD THE WAY.

NICE PLACE. SO THIS IS WHERE IT HAPPENS, EH?

GOOD EVENING. I'M ZACHARIAH KING. WHY DON'T YOU HAVE A SEAT, MR...?

THEY CALL ME SPIKE, ACTUALLY. LONG STORY. KINDA BLOODY, TOO.

Y'KNOW, I'M NOT SURPRISED I DIDN'T SMELL YOU BEFORE. WHAT WITH ALL THE RUCKUS DOWN THERE, AND YOU SMOKIN' THOSE BLOODY AW-FUL STOGIES TO COVER IT UP.

THIS CLOSE, THOUGH, THE STINK IS WRETCHED, MAKES ME WANT TO PUKE, REALLY.

NOT JUST THE STENCH, EITHER. YOU PATCHWORK DEMONS, ANYTHING FOR A BIT OF POWER, WORSHIPPIN' THIS ONE AND THAT. NEVER SEEN ANYTHING MORE STOMACH-TURNING.

YOU KNOW, I HAVE PLACES TO GO, PEOPLE TO EAT. IF YOU'RE THROUGH, I'LL HAVE MY MEN KILL YOU NOW.

IT'LL BE A BEAR GETTIN' THE ODOR OUT OF THIS ROOM.

DON'T FIGHT ME, VAMPIRE. ONE BITE, THAT'S ALL IT WILL TAKE.

DOING HIM A FAVOR, REALLY.

LISTEN TO ALL THOSE SCREAMS. THEY'RE LIKE MUSIC, BUT ONLY THE WIND INSTRUMENTS, THE PRETTIEST ONES.

DO YOU THINK THE SCREAMING ONES KNOW WHAT A MISTAKE YOU MADE, TRYING TO CHEAT MY SPIKE? I WANTED HIM TO HAVE A BIT OF FUN, AND YOU BOL LOCKSED IT ALL UP

IT HAPPENS. ONE LITTLE SLIP. ONE LITTLE NIBBLE, AND NOW THEY'VE GOT A TASTE FOR YOU AND YOUR... WHATEVER THE HELL THEY ARE.

KRIIICH TACH

SEE, ZACHARIAH, ONCE I FIG-URED OUT WHAT YOU WERE, AND PUT A LITTLE THOUGHT INTO IT--THE RIVER, YOUR POWER, IT ONLY MADE SENSE.

TEARS AND BLOOD AND RIVERS RUN... SOMETIMES ALL AT ONCE, EVERYONE KNOWS THAT.

IT'S ONE THING TO CALL UP AN ELEMENTAL DEMON, ANOTHER BLOODY THING ENTIRELY TO FLOAT YOUR HOUSE ON TOP OF IT, YOU'D HAVE TO BE AN IDIOT...

NOOOO!

BUT I GUESS YOU'VE GOT THAT COVERED.

SHLEKT

HEADING WEST.

DO YOU WANT TO LISTEN TO THE RADIO, SPIKE?

JUST A LITTLE PEACE AND QUIET AT THE MOMENT, DRU, ALL RIGHT?

ARE YOU MAD AT ME?

COULDN'T BE, PET. WASN'T YOUR FAULT. WE WANTED TO HAVE SOME FUN, DIDN'T WE? AND WE WILL, JUST AS SOON AS WE GET TO THE HELLMOUTH.

HIA873

OH, I CAN'T WAIT. IT'LL BE EVER SO MUCH FUN.

SPIKE?

YES, DRUSILLA?

I'M FAMISHED. YOU KNOW I CAN'T HEAR THE STARS WHEN I'M HUNGRY. DO YOU FANCY STOPPING FOR A BITE?

CICAGNE. A SMALL FISHING VILLAGE ON THE WESTERN COAST OF ITALY.

IT'S A SIMPLE LIFE. TO SOME, A PERFECT LIFE.

THE PEOPLE OF CICAGNE BELIEVE IN GOD, AND THE SEA.

AND WHEN THE SUN GOES DOWN, THERE ARE OTHER THINGS THEY BELIEVE.

WHICH IS WHY THEY DO NOT EVEN DISCUSS THIS SMALL COTTAGE, OR THE BRITISH COUPLE WHO HAVE BEEN LIVING HERE THESE PAST WEEKS.

THERE IS A LITTLE MANTRA THEY MUTTER, A WARD AGAINST WHAT LURKS IN THE NIGHT. TRANSLATED, IT MEANS, "DAWN ALWAYS COMES."

MUCH TO SPIKE'S CHAGRIN.

THIS IS JUST TOO MUCH.

DRUSILLA USED TO CALL SPIKE HER DARK PRINCE, AND HE WOULD TELL HER THAT HER SKIN TASTED LIKE OLIVES. THAT WAS A LONG TIME AGO. THAT WAS BEFORE...

...HE CAME BACK.

ANGEL. IT WOULD BE EASIER FOR SPIKE IF HE DIDN'T UNDERSTAND DRU'S OBSESSION WITH ANGEL. BUT HE DOES. ANGEL WAS DRUSILLA'S FIRST. HE MADE HER.

OH, YES, SPIKE UNDERSTANDS. FOR WHEN ANGEL TIRED OF DRUSILLA, HE FOUND ANOTHER FOR HER TO LOVE. DRU STOLE SPIKE'S LIFE, AND EVERY DAY SINCE.

SPIKE WAS MADE FOR HER.

HE UNDERSTANDS OBSESSION. BUT HE ALSO KNOWS THAT THE PAST IS PAST. DRUSILLA BELONGS TO HIM NOW, BODY AND DEMON-SOUL, AND HE BELONGS TO HER AS WELL.

SPIKE CAN'T SLEEP. BUT DRUSILLA SLEEPS DEEPLY THIS DAY. SLEEPS... AND DREAMS.

...OH, DARLING, THE MOON IS DOWN... CLOUDS SCREAMING BLACK RAIN... GIVE US A KISS...

MY BRAIN'S AWHIRL, PET, WE'VE GOT TO PUT THE PAST BEHIND US, PUT HIM BEHIND US, AND START AGAIN. WE NEED TO HAVE SOME FUN.

...ANGEL...

WAKE UP, DRU.

I SAID WAKE THE HELL UP! WE'VE JUST GOT IT BACK TOGETHER, PET...

OH, I AM A CLEVER GIRL. I FOUND HIM IN A FOREST ON THE ISLAND OF CRETE.

"YOU NEEDED TO BE PUNISHED. TO BE SPANKED. I KNOW YOU DON'T LIKE TO BE SPANKED."

WELL, THERE WAS THAT *ONE* TIME.

DON'T INTERRUPT.

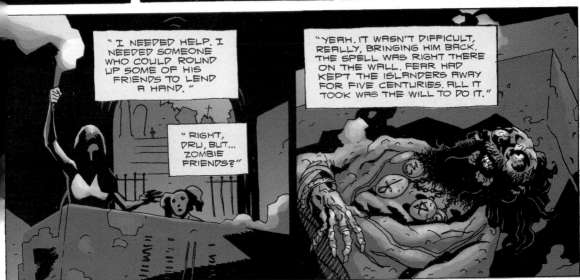

"I NEEDED HELP. I NEEDED SOMEONE WHO COULD ROUND UP SOME OF HIS FRIENDS TO LEND A HAND."

"RIGHT, DRU, BUT... ZOMBIE FRIENDS?"

"YEAH. IT WASN'T DIFFICULT, REALLY, BRINGING HIM BACK. THE SPELL WAS RIGHT THERE ON THE WALL. FEAR HAD KEPT THE ISLANDERS AWAY FOR FIVE CENTURIES. ALL IT TOOK WAS THE WILL TO DO IT."

THAT, AND THE BLOOD OF AN INNOCENT. SIMPLE AS THAT. MY OWN PET SORCERER.

DAMMIT, DRU, HOW COULD YOU? SO MUCH FOR ETERNITY, EH? WHAT DOES IT TAKE TO KEEP YOU HAPPY?

DO? I'LL HAVE YOUR GUTS FOR GARTERS, THAT'S WHAT I'LL DO.

MY BONES TURNED HOLLOW AND I FEARED I WOULD FLOAT AWAY. HE HELD ME DOWN. WHAT ARE *YOU* GOING TO DO ABOUT IT? REALLY, SPIKE, WHAT *CAN* YOU DO?

BUT FIRST THINGS FIRST.

KRASH!

A FUNGUS DEMON, DRU? THAT'S A NEW LOW.

IT WAS ONLY FOR PLAY, SPIKE. SOMETHING NEW. I WANTED TO GET DIRTY.

THAT'S WORSE, YOU SILLY COW. WHATEVER YOU THINK, I AM NOT YOUR DAMN PUPPY.

NO, YOU'RE THE BIG BAD, MY BAD BOY, AND I'VE BEEN A BAD GIRL, SO YOU MUST PUNISH ME.

SOD THAT. I'M DONE WITH YOU.

JUST UP THIS WAY, LOVE. I'D SAY YOU'RE JUST WHAT THE DOCTOR ORDERED. YOU'RE GOOD COMPANY, YOU ARE.

WHEN I'M ALONE ALL THE GHOSTS COME OUT TO PLAY. DREARY THINGS. AND ONLY THE SCREAMS CHASE THEM OFF.

BA-KOOM!

ALL MY PRETTY THINGS...

AND YOU...

...ANOTHER GHOST.

SPIKE.

NOT REALLY IN THE MOOD FOR A PARTY, ACTUALLY. BUT THAT'S ALWAYS THE BEST TIME TO HAVE ONE, ISN'T IT?

AND OLIVEIRA SAID IF I EVER NEEDED A PLACE TO STAY...

LOVELY OF YOU TO LET ME BORROW THE CAR, BY THE WAY.

DON'T WAIT UP.

OLIVEIRA?

LOOKS LIKE QUITE A PARTY.

YOU REALIZE YOU'VE RUINED RIO FOR ME NOW?

IT WAS THE LEAST I COULD DO.

CHAMPAGNE?

I'D BETTER NOT. IT MAKES ME ALL DIZZY.

WHAT HAPPENED, DRU?

YOU MADE ME TO BE WITH YOU, TO LOVE YOU. IF THAT WASN'T WHAT YOU WANTED, THEN WHY BOTHER?

POOR SPIKE, ALL ALONE. HAVEN'T YOU REALIZED IT YET? WE'RE ALL QUITE LONELY. ANGEL MADE ME AND THEN LEFT ME, ABANDONED ME.

IT'S WHAT WE DO. AND WHY WOULDN'T I? FACE IT, LOVE, YOU'VE LOST THE EDGE. YOU'RE JUST NOT *BAD* ENOUGH FOR ME ANYMORE.

DAMN YOU, DRU! STOP THIS! COME BACK TO ME AND WE'LL MAKE IT LIKE IT WAS!

OH? AND HOW WAS IT?

PERFECT, YOU AND ME, PET, LIKE ALWAYS. LIVING FOR EACH OTHER.

MEMORY SHIFTS WITH THE COLOR OF THE SKY. THE WORLD IS FULL OF PRETTINESS AND PAIN, AND IT CALLS ME. I DON'T LIVE FOR YOU, SPIKE.

THEN WHY, DRU? WHY THE HELL DID YOU MAKE ME?

JUST WANTED SOMEONE TO PLAY WITH, I GUESS.

BUT **WE** CAN STILL PLAY, SPIKE.

LIKE HELL.

I DON'T TAKE TABLE SCRAPS FROM ANYONE, DRU.

IT'S THE WHOLE FEAST OR NOTHING FOR ME.

THEN STARVE.

MEANWHILE, I LIKE IT HERE IN RIO. LOTS OF DEMONS, LOTS OF PARTIES, YOU CAN'T KILL THE WHOLE CITY.

NO.

GUESS I CAN'T.

IS THIS IT? THE HOUSE YOU TOLD US ABOUT? WITH THE VAMPIRE?

OH, VAMPIRES ALL RIGHT. AND MORE. GO TO IT, BOYS. THE EVIL THING'S JUST INSIDE.

YOU A FRIEND OF DRU'S, THEN? HEH.

SHE'LL LIVE, OF COURSE. SHE'LL KILL 'EM ALL. BUT AFTER TONIGHT SHE WON'T BE ABLE TO STAY IN RIO ANYMORE. LEAST I TOOK THAT AWAY FROM HER.

SORRY. JUST THINK I NEED A LITTLE TIME TO MY-SELF.

Stake out these Buffy the Vampire Slayer and Angel trade paperbacks

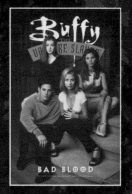

BUFFY THE VAMPIRE SLAYER

THE DUST WALTZ
Brereton • Gomez
80-page color paperback
ISBN: 1-84023-057-6

THE REMAINING SUNLIGHT
Watson • Van Meter
Bennett • Ross • Ketcham
88-page color paperback
ISBN: 1-84023-078-9

ALIENS

FEMALE WAR
(formerly Aliens: Earth War)
Verheiden • Kieth
112-page color paperback
ISBN: 1-85286-784-1

GENOCIDE
Arcudi • Willis • Story
112-page color paperback
ISBN: 1-85286-805-8

HARVEST
(formerly Aliens: Hive)
Prosser • Jones
128-page color paperback
ISBN: 1-85286-838-4

LABYRINTH
Woodring • Plunkett
136-page color paperback
ISBN: 1-85286-844-9

NIGHTMARE ASYLUM
(formerly Aliens: Book Two)
Verheiden • Beauvais
112-page color paperback
ISBN: 1-85286-765-5

OUTBREAK
(formerly Aliens: Book One)
Verheiden • Nelson
168-page color paperback
ISBN: 1-85286-756-6

ROGUE
Edginton • Simpson
112-page color paperback
ISBN: 1-85286-851-1

STRONGHOLD
Arcudi • Mahnke • Palmiotti
112-page color paperback
ISBN: 1-85286-875-9

ALIENS VS PREDATOR

ALIENS VS PREDATOR
Stradley • Norwood • Warner
Story • Campanella
176-page color paperback
ISBN: 1-85286-413-3

*THE DEADLIEST
OF THE SPECIES*
Claremont • Guice • Barreto
320-page color paperback
ISBN: 1-85286-953-4

WAR
Various
200-page color paperback
ISBN: 1-85286-703-5

BATMAN VS PREDATOR

BATMAN VS PREDATOR
Gibbons • Kubert • Kubert
96-page color paperback
ISBN: 1-85286-446-X

*BATMAN VS PREDATOR II:
BLOODMATCH*
Moench• Gulacy • Austin
136-page color paperback
ISBN: 1-85286-667-5

*BATMAN VS PREDATOR III:
BLOOD TIES*
Dixon • Damaggio
136-page color paperback
ISBN: 1-85286-913-5

GODZILLA

AGE OF MONSTERS
various
256-page B&W paperback
ISBN: 1-85286-929-1

PAST PRESENT FUTURE
various
276-page B&W paperback
ISBN: 1-85286-930-5

PREDATOR

BIG GAME
Arcudi • Dorkin • Gil
112-page color paperback
ISBN: 1-85286-454-0

COLD WAR
Verheiden • Randall • Mitchell
112-page color paperback
ISBN: 1-85286-576-8

KINDRED
Lamb • Tolson
112-page color paperback
ISBN: 1-85286-908-9

STAR WARS

CRIMSON EMPIRE
Richardson • Stradley
Gulacy • Russell
160-page color paperback
ISBN: 1-84023-006-1

*TALES OF THE JEDI: THE
GOLDEN AGE OF THE SITH*
Anderson • Gossett
Carrasco • Heike • Black Beckett •
Woch
144-page color paperback
ISBN: 1-84023-000-2

*X-WING ROGUE SQUADRON:
THE WARRIOR PRINCESS*
Stackpole • Tolson
Nadeau • Ensign
96-page color paperback
ISBN: 1-85286-997-6

*X-WING ROGUE SQUADRON:
REQUIEM FOR A ROGUE*
Stackpole • Strnad • Erskine
112-page color paperback
ISBN: 1-85286-026-6

VARIOUS

BATMAN/ALIENS
Marz • Wrightson
128-page color paperback
ISBN: 1-85286-887-2

*PREDATOR VS
JUDGE DREDD*
Wagner • Alcatena
80-page color paperback
ISBN: 1-84023-021-5

STARSHIP TROOPERS
various
144-page color paperback
ISBN: 1-85286-886-4

SUPERMAN/ALIENS
Jurgens • Nowlan
152-page color paperback
ISBN: 1-85286-704-3

*TARZAN VS PREDATOR
AT THE EARTH'S CORE*
Simonson • Weeks
104-page color paperback
ISBN: 1-85286-888-0

All publications are available through most good bookshops or direct from our mail-
order service at Titan Books. For a free
graphic-novels catalogue or to order, telephone 01858 433 169 with your credit-card
details or contact Titan Books Mail Order, Bowden House, 36 Northampton Road,
Market Harborough, Leics, LE16 9HE, quoting reference BSD/GN.